PUFFIN BOOKS

DIARY OF A WIMPY KID

WRECKING BALL

THE *DIARY OF A WIMPY KID* SERIES

MORE *DIARY OF A WIMPY KID* BOOKS

DIARY
of a
Wimpy Kid
WRECKING BALL

by Jeff Kinney

PUFFIN

PUFFIN BOOKS

UK | USA | Canada | Ireland | Australia
India | New Zealand | South Africa

Puffin Books is part of the Penguin Random House group of companies whose
addresses can be found at global.penguinrandomhouse.com.

www.penguin.co.uk   www.puffin.co.uk   www.ladybird.co.uk

First published in the English language in the USA
by Amulet Books, an imprint of ABRAMS, 2019
Original English title: *Diary of a Wimpy Kid: Wrecking Ball*
(All rights reserved in all countries by Harry N. Abrams, Inc.)
Published simultaneously in Great Britain by Puffin Books 2019

This edition published 2020

005

Book design by Jeff Kinney
Cover design by Chad W. Beckerman and Jeff Kinney

The moral right of the author/illustrator has been asserted

Printed at Thomson Press India Ltd, New Delhi

A CIP catalogue record for this book is available from the British Library

ISBN: 978-0-241-42669-2

All correspondence to:
Puffin Books, Penguin Random House Children's
One Embassy Gardens, 8 Viaduct Gardens, London SW11 7BW

MIX
Paper from
responsible sources
FSC
www.fsc.org   FSC® C018179

Penguin Random House is committed to a
sustainable future for our business, our readers
and our planet. This book is made from Forest
Stewardship Council® certified paper.

TO SCOOTER

MARCH

<u>Sunday</u>

I've read that in ancient times they used to bury kings and pharaohs with all their possessions. Back then I guess they thought you could take your things WITH you into the afterlife.

Well, if I get buried with all MY junk, I might really REGRET it later on.

Mom's having me do some spring cleaning to get rid of things I don't NEED. Well, that seemed like a good idea until I realized just how much stuff I've actually GOT.

I spent the whole morning going through my closet, and it's crazy how much was packed in there. And it's not like it was ORGANIZED or anything. I've basically been throwing things in my closet since we first moved in.

Digging through my closet was like going through my CHILDHOOD. And the further back I went, the further back in TIME it took me.

The stuff near the front of the closet was all junk I tossed in there over the past year, like homework and comic books. But after I got those things out of the way I started finding stuff I'D FORGOTTEN about.

I found a model rocket I got for my tenth birthday and a costume I wore for Halloween a few years ago. And there was a bunch of other things I didn't even know I still had.

When I dug a little DEEPER, I found something I thought I'd lost YEARS ago. It was a binder full of stickers I'd collected in the third grade.

I used to be OBSESSED with stickers, especially the scratch-and-sniff kind. I collected all the GOOD smells, like bubble gum and candyfloss and that sort of thing, but I had all the really GROSS ones, too.

So, when a kid on my street wanted to know what giraffe poop or rotten meat loaf smelled like, they'd come to ME.

One of these days I'm gonna write my AUTOBIOGRAPHY, and it's gonna include scratch-and-sniff stickers to mark all the different moments in my life.

I kept digging through my closet and found stuff from KINDERGARTEN, like a fish I made by tracing my hand on to a piece of card.

I used to LOVE doing arts and crafts back then. And, if anyone ever tried to BULLY me about it, they'd get a face full of glitter.

Another project I found in my closet was a gift I made for my mom in pre-school but never gave her. It was a paper flower with a picture of my face in the middle, glued to a popsicle stick.

When I made the thing, I put it in a little plant pot filled with earth. But I tripped on the front step when I got home from school that day, and that's why I never gave it to her.

I was GLAD when I finally reached the back of my closet, but, to be honest, I was a little DISAPPOINTED, too.

When I was younger I read this book about these kids who could visit a whole different WORLD by going through their wardrobe, and I always wondered if I might be able to do the same thing with MINE.

But I thought that whoever lived on the other side might not be too happy with me for tossing all my JUNK in there over the years.

When I told Mom I was done emptying my closet today, she said I needed to put everything into three piles: one to keep, one to donate and one to throw away. But I figured if I had to let go of any of my junk I might as well make some MONEY from it. So I decided to have a YARD SALE.

Mom thought that was a GREAT idea. So she gave me a magazine that had all sorts of tips on how to do it RIGHT.

All the ideas in the magazine were corny and old-fashioned, though. There was one section on how to create a sign to get people to come to your yard sale, and all the examples they showed were really BORING.

I knew that if I wanted people to actually show up at my yard sale I needed to do something a little more EYE-CATCHING. So I whipped up a sign I knew would do the trick.

$100 BILL

FOUND ON PAVEMENT

PLEASE COME TO
12 SURREY STREET
TO CLAIM YOUR PROPERTY

I made a few copies of my sign and headed out to post them around the neighbourhood. But Mom stopped me before I got out of the front door.

Mom made me make signs that were more like the ones in the magazine, and after I was finished, I stapled them to some telephone poles on our street. Then I hauled everything down from my bedroom and started setting it all out on some plastic tables.

Each table had its own category, like "clothes" and "books" and that kind of thing. But some stuff wasn't easy to categorize, so I had to get creative.

I had a bunch of gifts from my grandparents and older relatives that I've never even TOUCHED, so I put all those things together on one table.

Great Gifts
FOR YOUR
Grandkids

I also had a bunch of birthday cards that were still in pretty good shape. So I used some Tippex to cover up my name and set them out on their own table.

I put all my broken toys on another table and hoped some little kids who couldn't READ would come to the yard sale.

I stuffed all my random items, like marbles and a few pencil stubs, into some socks and pinned them to a table.

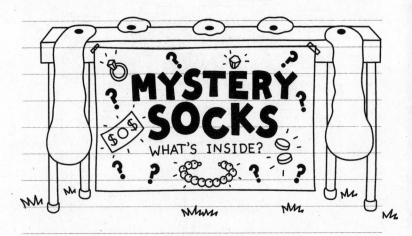

I also created a table full of things for people who had money to burn.

I put all my old arts-and-crafts projects on their own table, just in case some kids needed a gift for their parents but didn't want to put in the TIME.

While I was finishing up, Mom came outside to check out my yard sale, and she seemed pretty IMPRESSED. But she said I should hold on to the things I'd made myself, since that stuff is really SPECIAL.

I told Mom that if she wanted something, she could always buy it HERSELF. So she offered me three dollars for that paper flower I'd made for her in pre-school.

Mom seemed pretty eager to have that thing, and I could tell it was worth more than three bucks to her. So I told Mom it was all hers for TEN.

I guess I pushed my luck, though, because she went back inside without buying ANYTHING.

While I waited for customers to show up, I started getting a little NERVOUS. I realized that all my stuff was just lying out in the open, and I had no way to stop people from STEALING it.

So I called my best friend, Rowley Jefferson, and asked him to come down and be my Theft Prevention Officer.

But Rowley said he was supposed to do something with his dad this afternoon, so he couldn't help me with the yard sale.

I told him I'd promote him to Theft Prevention MANAGER, and he'd even get to wear a BADGE. Luckily, that did the trick.

As soon as Rowley got to my house, he started asking about that BADGE. All I could find was my old firefighter costume, but that seemed to make him feel important.

Rowley asked what he was supposed to DO as the Theft Prevention Manager, and I said mostly he needed to walk around and crack his knuckles to make sure nobody got any funny ideas.

But Rowley wasn't paying any attention to my instructions, because he was distracted by a table that had a bunch of birthday gifts he'd got me over the years.

I'm pretty sure Rowley's MOM picks out my presents, since they're always things that help you LEARN. And they're all still in mint condition, because I haven't actually OPENED any of them.

I don't know what made Rowley madder, the fact that I was SELLING this stuff or the sign I put on the table.

Rowley said I couldn't sell those things because they were GIFTS. I told him they were MINE, so I could do whatever I WANTED with them. And then we got into a big tug-of-war over the Magnet Fun set.

That's when our first customers started to arrive. I told Rowley we could argue about this LATER, but for NOW we needed to act like PROFESSIONALS.

At first just a few people showed up, but after a while a lot MORE came. And, when they started checking out my stuff, I went into sales mode.

THE CRAFTSMANSHIP ON THIS PORCUPINE IS REMARKABLE!

QUALITY ARTS & CRAFTS

One lady seemed interested in a collector's coin I got from my uncle, but she complained that it was DENTED. So I thought fast and told her the REASON it was dented was because it had stopped a bullet in the Second World War.

She didn't seem to BELIEVE me, though, probably because the coin was dated last year.

I spent a lot of time trying to close that deal, and I started worrying that people were stealing behind my back. Unfortunately my Theft Prevention Manager was totally useless, because he was busy playing with the magnet set.

I told Rowley he'd better start doing his JOB or he was gonna get FIRED. But Rowley said it wasn't a REAL job anyway, because he wasn't getting PAID.

I explained that I hadn't SOLD anything yet and didn't have any MONEY to pay him with. So when he said he was LEAVING I told him he could pick out one item from any table and THAT could be his payment.

Rowley seemed pretty excited about that idea, and I thought for SURE he'd choose the magnet set. But he headed straight for the Rare Items table instead.

I explained that those things were for PAYING customers ONLY and that maybe he'd be interested in something from the Fun Toys table. But Rowley wouldn't BUDGE.

Eventually he settled on the Vampire Bat Shield. And I was OK with that, because it was really just a broken umbrella. But now Rowley was so worried about BATS that he couldn't concentrate on his job.

While Rowley was fooling around with his stupid umbrella, I thought I saw a guy take an action figure from the Collectibles table and stuff it in his pocket. So I ran over to deal with him.

But the only things in the guy's pockets were some used tissues and car keys.

I was glad I was staying ALERT, though, because I headed off a major DISASTER. A pickup truck pulled up at the kerb, and some guy from Whirley Street started piling my stuff into the back.

I asked him what he was DOING, and he said that since tomorrow was trash day he thought the stuff by the kerb was up for grabs.

But I didn't have time to explain the concept of a yard sale to this guy, because all of a sudden I had an even BIGGER problem to deal with.

It started to RAIN, and everyone was heading back to their cars.

I was worried I might never get this many people to come to a yard sale again, and I wanted to sell SOMETHING to make all the effort worth it. So I went round and marked down the prices on every item.

Then it started REALLY raining, and I knew I was gonna have to do something DRASTIC.

I threw a bunch of stuff into BOXES, and offered even BIGGER discounts. But by then it was too late anyway.

I knew that if I didn't get my stuff inside it was all gonna get RUINED. So I asked Rowley to hold his umbrella over my most valuable items while I ran everything else into the garage.

But Rowley wasn't any help at all.

He said his shift had just ended and it was time for him to go home.

So I was on my own. I tried carrying a box of comic books into the garage, but by now the box was SOGGY, and the bottom gave way.

It took me about a hundred trips to get everything into the garage. But I probably shouldn't have even BOTHERED, because most of my stuff was already RUINED.

I figured I could still make ONE sale, though. I told Mom that the paper flower was all hers for three bucks. Unfortunately by then she'd changed her mind.

<u>Wednesday</u>

I'm actually kind of GLAD nobody bought anything from my yard sale the other day, because if I ever get FAMOUS that stuff is gonna be worth a LOT more money than I was asking for it.

I'd feel pretty dumb if I sold one of my old homework projects for fifty cents and then someone auctioned it off later for a few thousand dollars.

One day they'll probably make my childhood home into one of those places schools visit on field trips.

And if THAT happens they're gonna want to have all the authentic stuff I owned growing up.

The reason I'm not ALREADY famous is because when you're a kid they keep you busy with school and homework, so there's not a lot of time left to make a NAME for yourself.

But one of the ways a kid can actually get famous is by becoming a HERO. My parents watch the news every night, and there's always a story about a kid saving someone from choking or something like that.

The problem is, those kinds of opportunities don't come around that OFTEN. And, believe me, I've tried to put myself in the right place for that sort of thing to happen.

But I've got kind of tired of WAITING, so I decided to try and create a situation where I was GUARANTEED to be a hero. I figured if I saved someone from a dog attack they'd make a statue of me and put it in the town park, which would be pretty cool.

Rowley didn't seem so sure about my idea when I explained it to him. But when I said he'd be a part of the statue, too, he changed his tune.

So I got some bacon out of our refrigerator and had Rowley stuff it in his pockets. Then we went around the neighbourhood looking for some DOGS.

We DID attract some dogs, but they weren't the kind I was LOOKING for.

Rowley got so nervous about the dogs following us that he ATE the uncooked bacon, which I've heard can be really BAD for you. So I told his parents what happened, and they took him to a doctor just to be sure.

I guess I saved Rowley's life after all, which does sort of make me a hero, if you think about it. But I don't know if that's really the kind of thing they make into a statue.

Maybe I'm thinking too SMALL with this statue idea, anyway. If I do something REALLY big, they'll make my birthday into a national holiday.

That would be pretty awesome, because then everyone will get the day off school and work, and they'll have ME to thank for it.

The thing is, whenever there's a day off school for a national holiday, I never even THINK about the person it's named after. I just hope that on MY holiday people will spend the whole day reflecting on my life.

But with MY luck they'll just use it as an opportunity to sell furniture or something.

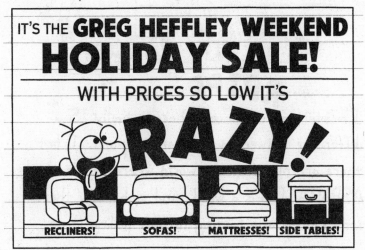

IT'S THE **GREG HEFFLEY WEEKEND HOLIDAY SALE!**
WITH PRICES SO LOW IT'S

RAZY!

RECLINERS! SOFAS! MATTRESSES! SIDE TABLES!

APRIL

<u>Sunday</u>

All the rain we've been getting has been making everything grow like crazy. And that really stinks, because it's MY job to weed our garden.

I don't know why Mom gave me this job, because she knows I'm BAD at it. I can't tell the difference between a weed and something that's SUPPOSED to be in the garden, and I keep ripping up the wrong stuff by mistake.

I'm still not convinced there actually IS a difference between a weed and a plant. I bet there are places in the world where people think ASPARAGUS is a weed, and right now there's some kid my age busting his gut pulling it up.

I don't understand why GRASS isn't considered a weed, because it sure looks like one to ME. But people like my dad spend their entire weekends trying to get their lawn to look just right so they can impress their neighbours.

I'll tell you this: when I get a place of my OWN, I'm gonna PAVE the whole yard. That way I can spend my weekends ENJOYING myself.

I'm gonna save a TON of money by paving the yard. My dad spends a FORTUNE on lawn fertilizer, and I don't think that stuff's GOOD for you. And the proof is my neighbour Fregley, who's always out in his yard right after they spray.

I'm pretty sure all those lawn chemicals can mess with your GENES. So if I end up with a third eye or something, I'm gonna blame my PARENTS.

When I have my own place, EVERYTHING'S gonna be different. And I'm not just talking about the LAWN, either.

I USED to think I wanted to live in a big mansion with a giant fence around it. But then I realized that if I was famous, everyone would know where I LIVED.

So my NEW plan is to build a really SMALL house that doesn't attract a lot of attention. And then all the GOOD stuff will be UNDERGROUND.

I've got ideas for what's gonna go on each level. In fact, I just finished designing the fifth floor last week, and it's probably my FAVOURITE.

TRAMPOLINE PARK

ROTATING RESTAURANT

LASER TAG ARENA

BOWLING ALLEY

SECRET CANDY STASH

ARCADE

ARCHERY RANGE

I'm a little worried about living UNDERGROUND, though, because my brother Rodrick lives in our basement, and I'm not sure it's HEALTHY. So I'm gonna have tons of screens that LOOK like windows to make it feel like I'm living on the surface.

My house is gonna be BIG, so it'll take me a while to get from place to place. That's why I'm planning on having moving walkways everywhere.

My bathtub is gonna be made of glass, and it'll sit inside a giant aquarium so I can feel like I'm in the OCEAN.

My security system is gonna be SUPER high tech. I've designed all sorts of booby traps for anyone who tries to get inside.

And if someone gets past the front door I'll just wait them out in my panic room, which is gonna have steel walls that are three feet thick.

Every so often I'll probably have a party or something so people can see how awesome my house is. But if they stay too LATE I'll have a way to get them out of there and back up to street level.

All this stuff is gonna be EXPENSIVE, so it's going to take a while for me to save enough money to make it happen. But I figure it can't hurt to start planning NOW.

<u>Friday</u>
I was doing my homework last night when Dad called me downstairs. Mom was at the kitchen table, and she seemed pretty upset.

Dad told us Great Aunt Reba passed away in her sleep. I have a LOT of great aunts, though, and at first I couldn't remember which one she was.

Mom reminded me that Aunt Reba was the one who used to send me angry letters when I forgot to write her thank-you notes for my birthday money. And then I knew EXACTLY which one she was.

I guess MANNY remembered Aunt Reba, because he seemed pretty upset she had died.

So tonight Mom read him a book she'd read to ME when Meemaw passed away.

Mom has a whole SHELF of these Preston Platypus books, and each one covers a different topic. She'd pull one out every time I had to deal with something NEW.

When I found the books in Mom's closet, I read them all in one afternoon. I probably shouldn't have done that, though, because those books turned me into a nervous WRECK.

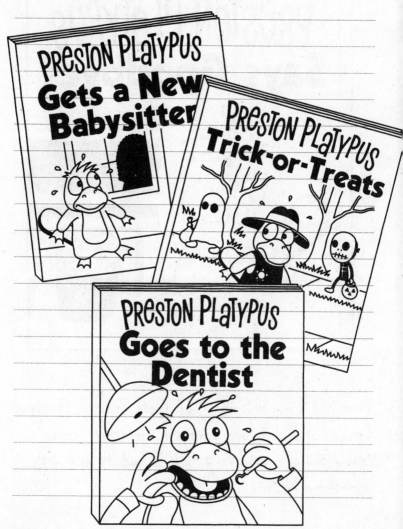

One of the books was about how Preston Platypus was sad that a tree in his yard died and had to be cut down. Well, when my parents said they needed to take down a dead tree in OUR yard, I was a total MESS.

So my parents decided NOT to chop it down. But then a few weeks later the tree fell down in a storm and took out half our deck.

CRRACKK

49

The Preston Platypus books all follow the same basic formula. At first, Preston's worried about something, and then his mom tells him things are gonna be OK, and she turns out to be RIGHT.

I guess the reason I kept reading those books was because I always hoped there would be a big TWIST at the end. And then I'd be disappointed when there WASN'T.

So I started coming up with my OWN endings to the books. And when Mom saw what I'd drawn in the back of "Preston Platypus Goes to the Zoo" she took me to see a counsellor.

<u>Saturday</u>
Today was Aunt Reba's funeral. Mom said we had
to go because Aunt Reba didn't have much family,
so we needed to show our support.

She told us we all had to wear BLACK to the
funeral, but when Rodrick came out wearing the
outfit he wore to his last rock concert Mom made
him go back inside and CHANGE.

That's why we were fifteen minutes late to the
funeral. When we got there, the service had already
started, so we just stood at the back behind a
crowd of people. I'd never been in a cemetery
for that LONG before, so I felt a little
NERVOUS.

That's because Rodrick always says that when you go past a cemetery you need to hold your breath so you don't swallow a GHOST. Well, I held my breath for as long as I COULD today, but there was no WAY I could make it through the whole funeral.

I just hope I didn't swallow any ghosts, because middle school is hard ENOUGH without being possessed by a person from the 1600s.

Some of the tombstones had quotes on them, and that got me thinking about what I want written on MINE. Hopefully I'll say something really WISE right before I die, and they'll carve my last words on to my tombstone.

But I'll probably say something really DUMB and they'll use it anyway.

HEFFLEY

"Does this have chickpeas in it? Because I'm allergic to chickpeas."

I've got a lot of questions about what happens to you after you die. For one thing, I wanna know how you LOOK in the afterlife.

53

If everyone's appearance is frozen when they pass away, then Heaven probably looks a lot like Leisure Towers.

I wanna know what you WEAR up in Heaven, too. If you're stuck in the clothes you had on just before you died, I seriously hope nothing bad happens to me on HALLOWEEN.

I'll tell you this: I wanna stay alive for as long as I can. But I wouldn't want to live FOREVER.

Whenever you see a movie about someone who becomes IMMORTAL, there's always a CATCH that totally ruins it.

THE GOOD NEWS IS, YOU'RE GONNA LIVE FOREVER!

GREAT!

THE BAD NEWS IS, YOU'RE A VAMPIRE AND YOU HAVE TO DRINK PEOPLE'S BLOOD TO SURVIVE.

PLUS, YOU CAN'T GO OUTSIDE IN DAYLIGHT.

DANG IT!

When a person is immortal, they always have to HIDE it from everyone else. I guess if people know you can't die they treat you like a MONSTER or something.

But if I was immortal I wouldn't even TRY to hide it. In fact, I'd mention it every chance I COULD.

MAKE SURE YOU FASTEN YOUR SEAT BELT!

YEAH, WELL, I CAN'T DIE, SO WHATEVER!

In school we learned about the world's religions and how everyone believes different things. In some places they believe that, when you die, you get reborn as someone ELSE.

Some people think you can come back as a totally different creature, like an animal or an insect or something. And WHAT you come back as depends on whether you were GOOD or BAD.

Well, that actually makes me a little worried, because I've done a few things in my life that I'm not proud of.

And if PLANTS have feelings, then I could REALLY be in trouble.

Hopefully there's still enough time for me to make things right. Because I seriously don't want to come back as a dung beetle in my next life.

Mom told us Aunt Reba didn't have a lot of family, but she did have lots of FRIENDS, which would explain why there were so many people at her funeral.

Well, I'd better start adding some new friends MYSELF, or I'm not gonna draw much of a crowd when it's all over for me.

When the service ended today, everyone started to leave. I thought I'd recognize SOME people, because I know that Aunt Reba had a couple of sisters who are still alive. But I didn't see ANYBODY I knew, which was weird.

Mom seemed confused, too. When the crowd thinned out, we made our way to the grave. And that's when we figured out we'd been at the WRONG FUNERAL.

By the time we got to Aunt Reba's grave, the ceremony was over and everyone was already gone.

All I can say is, I hope Aunt Reba was looking down from Heaven and having a good laugh about us missing her funeral. But, from what I remember about her, she wasn't really the type of person to have a good laugh about ANYTHING.

<u>Monday</u>
During dinner tonight, Mom said we needed to have a family meeting. And family meetings are never much FUN.

Mom told us Aunt Reba had lived a really humble life in a small apartment, but that she had been careful with her money and made some really smart investments. Well, I had NO idea why Mom was telling us all this.

But then came the big news. Mom said that Aunt Reba had left all her money to her FAMILY. And it took me a second to realize that included US.

Apparently, when you find out this sort of news you're not supposed to act HAPPY about it, because I guess that's disrespectful to the person who passed away. But nobody told us KIDS that.

After Mom got us to settle down, she said we needed to have a serious discussion about what to do with our INHERITANCE.

I already knew EXACTLY how I was gonna spend MY share.

Thanks Reba

Rodrick said he wanted to use HIS share to buy a tour bus for his band, and Dad wanted to buy some really expensive figurines for his Civil War diorama. Manny wanted to use HIS money to fill his bedroom with chocolate pudding for some reason.

But Mom shot down everyone's ideas. She said we were making this decision as a FAMILY, and whatever we did with the money was gonna have to benefit EVERYBODY.

Then she told us HER idea, which was to use the money for HOME IMPROVEMENTS.

Everyone else thought that was a really BORING idea, but not ME. I ran upstairs to get the blueprints for my dream house, and I went through them, floor by floor.

But Mom said the money Aunt Reba left us wouldn't even pay for the ice-skating rink I designed for the second level. So I tried out some of my LESS expensive ideas, like the couch with a built-in toilet.

FLUSH

PRESS

Mom wasn't crazy about THOSE ideas, either. She said she was thinking about using the money for an EXTENSION. Well, that sounded like a GREAT idea to ME. I figured if we added two more storeys to the top of our house, then everyone in the family could have their own FLOOR.

Rodrick wanted to make the extension into a recording studio, and Dad wanted to make it all glass so he could show off his Civil War diorama to the neighbours.

Manny had his OWN idea for what to put in the extension, but I think it was mostly just the chocolate-pudding thing again.

Of course Mom didn't like any of OUR ideas, and she said she had a totally DIFFERENT plan for what the extension should be.

Mom said she'd always wanted a bigger KITCHEN, and she was really excited to use the money for THAT.

None of us really liked that idea, though, and we kept brainstorming OTHER things we could put in there.

But now Mom was MAD. She said she was the only person in the family who'd ever sent Aunt Reba a thank-you note for anything, so SHE was gonna decide how to use the money. And, for some reason, that was the end of the conversation.

See, this is why leaving your relatives money is a bad idea. All it does is make everyone MISERABLE.

I'm not planning on leaving ANY money behind when I go. I'm gonna spend every last cent so there's nothing left for people to FIGHT over.

I can GUARANTEE that me and my brothers are gonna fight over whatever inheritance we get from Mom and Dad. And I'm ALREADY worried that I'm not gonna get my fair share.

That's because when I first learned to write my name Rodrick made me sign a bunch of pieces of paper. And who KNOWS what kinds of things I'd agreed to back then.

I promise to give Rodrick all my money.

Greg

I prom... clean Rodric... house.

Greg

...romise do all ...'s chores.

Greg

Greg

...pro... wash Rodrick car.

Greg

Greg

Rodrick always says he's the "firstborn" so he'll get our parents' house and all their MONEY, too. But I don't think it works like that any more.

If he's RIGHT, though, then I'm glad I'm the
SECOND in line and not the THIRD, because
Manny's got NO chance of getting any money
with two older brothers in front of him. And
that's the reason I always watch my back around
that kid.

MAY

<u>Saturday</u>

The great thing about this extension is that it gives me something to brag about to Rowley on our way to school.

I told him that our new kitchen is gonna have granite countertops and a tile floor and brand-new appliances. But, instead of getting JEALOUS, he acted HAPPY for me. So I don't understand what kind of game he's playing.

Rowley's house is newer than ours, and it's a lot BIGGER, too.

And that's not right, because Rowley's an only child, so he doesn't even NEED all that room.

Back when Rowley first moved in, I told him we should swap houses to make things more FAIR. Rowley thought that was a good idea, but unfortunately his dad DIDN'T. And I think that's what got me and Mr Jefferson off on the wrong foot.

Anyway, I'm actually getting kind of EXCITED for construction to begin, because it's gonna be NICE having some more space. But I guess they've gotta do a bunch of paperwork before they can get started for real.

Dad wants to fix a few things around the house before construction begins anyway, and he wants me and Rodrick to HELP him.

Dad says once me and Rodrick get our OWN places we're gonna have to know how to do repairs OURSELVES. I keep telling Dad that by the time we're HIS age we won't HAVE to fix things ourselves. But he never seems to want to hear it.

Whenever Dad tries to teach me how to do something new, I always have trouble following him. A couple of weeks ago he showed me and Rodrick how to change a tyre, but I guess I lost interest when he started talking about lug nuts and air pressure.

Dad was frustrated that I wasn't paying attention, and he asked me what I'm gonna do if I ever get stuck by the side of the road with a flat tyre. I told him I'm planning on buying a WHISTLE, and I'll just blow it if I ever need help.

I guess that was the wrong answer, though, because since then Dad's been on my case to learn how to do things for MYSELF.

Today Dad said he was gonna teach me how to "snake a drain", which didn't sound like fun to ME. And when I found out it was a PLUMBING thing, I got SCARED.

I've had a fear of plumbing ever since I was a little kid. It's all because I overheard Mom talking to Dad outside my bedroom just after we moved in.

THE GROUT IN THIS BATHROOM IS REALLY NASTY!

What I didn't know THEN was that grout is the gritty stuff between the bathroom tiles. But, when Mom said that word, it put a picture in my mind.

Since I'd never SEEN the Grout, I figured it must hide in the pipes whenever I walked into the bathroom. So that made me nervous around taps and drains.

I was scared that one day the Grout was gonna grab one of my ankles when I was in the shower and pull me down the drain.

And I didn't feel safe in Mom and Dad's bathroom, either, because I figured the Grout could just slither through the pipes and get me in THERE if it wanted to.

I thought maybe I could at least stop the Grout from getting out of the taps by BLOCKING them. So one day I went around the house putting balloons over all the nozzles, which turned out to be a pretty dumb move now that I think about it.

ZIP

BLOOSH

I knew I needed a way to DEFEND myself if the Grout ever came after me while I was using the bathroom. And I found the perfect weapon in the cabinet underneath the sink.

From then on, if I was in the bathroom, I was ARMED.

But later I started to worry that the Grout might slip out of the bathroom and get me in my BEDROOM.

And a few times I was sure it was actually right there in the room WITH me.

But when I woke up in the morning the Grout was GONE.

BLINK
BLINK

Finally, I told Mom I was too scared to sleep alone because I was afraid of the Grout.

Mom thought the whole thing was HILARIOUS and showed me what grout REALLY was.

Then she told me that a monster is only real if you BELIEVE in it, and if I stopped thinking the Grout was real it would DISAPPEAR.

I realized that was EXACTLY what the Grout would WANT me to think, and I wondered if the Grout was actually pretending to be MOM.

So, from that point on, I kept my bedroom door LOCKED, just in case.

Eventually I guess I DID stop believing in the
Grout. Well, at least until TODAY when Dad
unclogged the drain and pulled out a glob of
HAIR. And, for ME, that's all the proof I
NEEDED.

I spent the rest of the day locked in my room.
And that was where I planned on STAYING,
at least until Dad took my door off the hinges
with a screwdriver.

I didn't even know you could DO that. So Dad
should be happy, because he actually taught me
something NEW today.

<u>Sunday</u>

This morning Dad woke me and Rodrick up early and told us we had to go with him to the DIY store. He said he had a day of chores lined up for us, and we needed to get some supplies.

It's been a while since we went to the DIY store, and the last time we were there we got kicked out. That's because Manny used the toilet on the display floor.

Dad went to find stuff to fix the washing machine, and he sent me and Rodrick to get some other things, like wood stain and paintbrushes.

I'll tell you this: if there's ever a zombie invasion or something like that, I'm heading STRAIGHT for the DIY store. Because there's stuff in there that can do some SERIOUS damage.

RRRRRR

When we got back home, Dad told me and Rodrick we were gonna stain the deck. He said we'd have to paint around the hot tub since it was too heavy to move.

Honestly, I wish we never GOT the hot tub, because that thing has been nothing but TROUBLE.

This winter the hot tub almost KILLED me, not ONCE but TWICE.

One night we had a big storm, and the strap holding down the hot-tub cover came undone. So Dad told me I had to get out there and FIX it.

After I got on all my winter gear, I went outside to deal with this thing. The cover was flapping around like CRAZY, and it wasn't easy trying to wrestle it back down. And, just when I thought I HAD it, a big gust of wind came and blew the cover clear off the deck.

But I was still holding on to the cover, so I went flying WITH it.

If there hadn't been three feet of SNOW on the ground, that would've been IT for me.

After I checked to make sure I didn't have any broken bones, I dragged the cover through the snow and up the stairs. And by the time I got to the TOP I was completely EXHAUSTED.

But that's not the end of the story. The hose
Dad used to FILL the hot tub was running down
the stairs, and it was frozen SOLID. So when I
STEPPED on the hose, I slid all the way back
down to the BOTTOM and almost broke my neck
on the landing.

Rodrick's had problems with the hot tub, too. He
used it all winter, but had a bad habit of falling
ASLEEP in it. So Mom would always have to make
sure he wasn't still outside when she went to bed
for the night.

But one time Mom forgot to check on Rodrick before she went to sleep and didn't realize he was out there until the MORNING.

It took something like two WEEKS for Rodrick's skin to smooth out so he could stop looking like a PRUNE. And during that time his high school had their yearbook photos taken.

Rodrick Heffley

A few months back Dad drained the hot tub, and there hasn't been any water in it SINCE. I'm just hoping we get RID of that thing before it causes any SERIOUS damage.

While we were staining the deck near the hot tub today, I heard a buzzing noise and thought maybe someone had accidentally left the heater running.

So I lifted the cover to check. And, as soon as I DID, I knew I was in TROUBLE.

Some wasps had made a NEST underneath the cover, and now they were all stirred up. If I made a sudden move, I was gonna get STUNG. I didn't know what to DO, but Rodrick made the decision FOR me.

The wasps went BERSERK, and I dropped the hot-tub cover, then RAN for it. Somehow me and Rodrick BOTH managed to get inside without getting stung.

We were really lucky, because I've read that wasps can sting you MULTIPLE times, unlike a regular honeybee, which can only sting you ONCE.

I wonder what it's like knowing that, if you sting someone, you'll DIE. If I was a honeybee, I'd be tempted to use my stinger every DAY. ESPECIALLY if I was surrounded by bees my age.

But if I went through my whole life without ever using my stinger I'm sure I'd end up REGRETTING it.

NOOO...

This afternoon Dad wanted to know why me and Rodrick weren't still outside staining the back deck. Rodrick told him about the WASPS, but left out the part about spraying their nest with the hose.

Then Dad said he had another job for us in the FRONT yard. He said the gutters were clogged and needed cleaning, so we had to go and get the ladder out of the garage.

Cleaning the gutters is my LEAST favourite chore, because it's always ME who has to climb up the ladder.

Dad won't do it any more because the LAST time he did he had a run-in with a SQUIRREL.

So now RODRICK won't go up the ladder, either. He says the person who's LIGHTEST has to do it, because they won't get hurt as badly if they FALL.

Rodrick even drew a diagram to show me the science behind it. And, if that was supposed to make me feel BETTER, it DIDN'T.

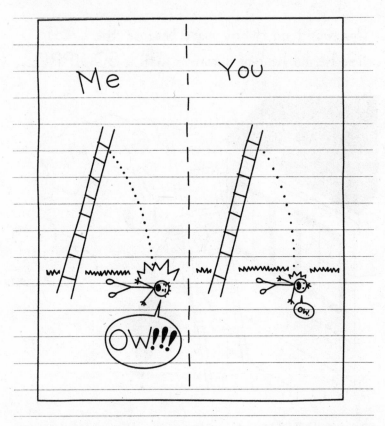

We got the ladder out of the garage and carried it to the front yard. Then we leaned it against the roof, and Rodrick held the base in place so I could climb up.

When I got to the top, I started scooping the muddy slop from the gutters into the trash bag I was holding in my other hand. That meant I couldn't really hold on to the ladder, and it was hard to keep my balance.

After I cleared out that section, I climbed back down and we moved the ladder to another spot. But, on my fourth trip up, I noticed the ladder felt a little more WOBBLY than usual.

I yelled down to Rodrick to hold the ladder STEADY, but I didn't get any response. And, when I looked to see if he was on his phone or something, he wasn't even THERE.

And that's when I looked through the bathroom window and saw Rodrick INSIDE THE HOUSE.

I knocked on the glass to get his attention. But I must've leaned over too FAR, because the ladder started tilting to one side.

It was too late for me to try and climb all the way back down, so the only place to go was UP.

I climbed to the top of the ladder and grabbed the edge of the roof with both hands, then pulled myself up on to it. I did it just in time, too, because the second I stepped off the ladder it went crashing to the ground.

So now I was stuck on the roof with no way to get back down. I yelled out, hoping Mom or Dad would hear me. But I was pretty sure Dad was in the laundry room fixing the washing machine, and I hadn't seen MOM all morning.

Then I spotted Mr Larocca driving his lawn mower out of his shed, and I thought I was SAVED. I tried SHOUTING to him, but he couldn't hear me over the sound of the mower.

I figured I could get Mr Larocca's attention by throwing some of the gloop from the gutters in front of his mower to get him to stop and look up.

So I scooped up some sludge and aimed for a spot in Mr Larocca's path. But I guess I miscalculated a little, because I nailed the mower with a direct HIT.

And, believe me, I couldn't make that shot again if I had a HUNDRED more goes.

SPLAP

Mr Larocca stopped his mower and tried to figure out where the ambush had COME from. I decided maybe it wasn't so bad to be stuck on the roof AFTER all, and I scrambled over to the other side where he wouldn't be able to see me.

I hid behind the chimney, which was the only shady place on the roof. And even there it was pretty HOT.

I knew I could be in for a long wait, and after a while I started worrying about getting DEHYDRATED.

So I took off most of my clothes, because I didn't want to SWEAT too much. I thought that if I got really desperate I might be able to wring some moisture out of my SOCKS. But I was really hoping it wouldn't come to that.

I knew that if I didn't do something to save myself they'd eventually find me in one of those satellite photos.

It was too far to jump DOWN, so that was out of the question. And, even if I landed on the back deck without killing myself, those wasps would probably finish me off.

Then I remembered there was a window on the side of the house above the garage. So I lowered myself down from the roof and on to the ledge, which was BARELY within reach.

Luckily, the window wasn't LOCKED. I opened it just wide enough for me to fit inside, and I squeezed through.

The window led to Mom and Dad's bathroom, and the ledge was right above their TOILET.

I put one foot down on top of the cistern, and then I tried to put my OTHER foot down on top of the toilet LID. But I didn't notice the seat was UP until it was too LATE.

So now my ankle was STUCK, and I couldn't pull my foot out, no matter how hard I tried. I guess I was making a lot of noise trying to get myself free, because that was when I found out where MOM had been all this time.

And it really wasn't fun explaining the situation to Dad when HE came into the bathroom.

So it wasn't a great day for me. But the good news is, Mom said that from now on we're getting our gutters cleaned by PROFESSIONALS.

Tuesday

It turns out I'm not the ONLY one who got replaced by someone who actually knows what they're doing. It happened to DAD, too.

Dad took the washing machine apart but couldn't put it back together. So Mom made him hire a plumber to fix it.

It's been really inconvenient living without a washing machine. We've had to wash our clothes by hand in the kitchen sink, which is a big pain. But Rodrick came up with a SHORT CUT last night and put his dirty clothes in the DISHWASHER.

Well, the dishwasher did a good job WASHING the clothes, but not DRYING them.

And, when Rodrick left the house to go to school this morning, his clothes were still WET.

So he used his van to AIR-DRY his clothes on the way to school.

LÖDED DIPER

Unfortunately for Rodrick, that got the attention of the POLICE, who pulled him over.

That's why Mom made Dad call someone to fix the washing machine. But I didn't know the plumber was in the house until I walked past the laundry room.

The guy must've known what he was DOING, because he got the washing machine up and running.

But things ended kind of awkwardly when Manny
tried to pay the plumber using Mom's credit card.

Wednesday

When I came home from school this afternoon,
there were a bunch of builders and heavy machinery
in our yard.

I was super EXCITED, because that meant this extension was finally happening for REAL.

A guy was using a digger to excavate the hole for the foundations, and it was CRAZY to see how POWERFUL that thing was.

Me and Rowley tried to dig a hole to China once, and we quit after a few hours. But if we could've got our hands on one of THESE things we might've actually pulled it off.

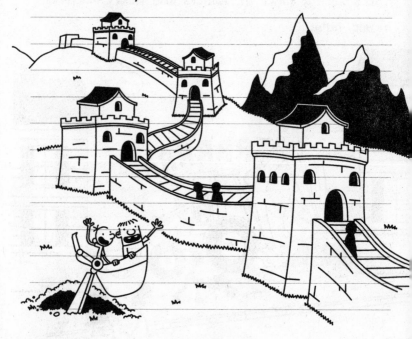

I'm wondering if the crew would let me take the digger out for a SPIN. Because I could use it to pull the most epic prank EVER at my school.

It was pretty hot today, and I think Mom felt sorry for the guys who were working hard. So she made some cold drinks and took them outside.

It kind of backfired, though, because after that the builders started coming inside to use the TOILET.

And when a line formed for the DOWNSTAIRS toilet, the biggest guy on the construction crew headed UPSTAIRS to find another one.

And that guy was carrying a MAGAZINE, so I got the feeling he wasn't heading up there to go and do a Number One.

I wanted to try and STOP him, so I pressed the "test" button on the smoke detector to set it off.

The builders all got out of our house pretty QUICK, but they weren't the ONLY ones who thought there was an actual emergency.

MANNY thought so, too. And, when the smoke detector went off, he threw all his stuffed animals out of his bedroom window, then hopped on to the pile.

SPROING

Mom and Dad weren't happy with me for the smoke-detector thing, but I don't think they were crazy about the builders using our toilets, EITHER. So this evening Mom ordered one of those porta-potties for the work site, and now everybody's happy.

Friday
Yesterday the construction crew poured concrete for the foundations, and today they started on the framing for the extension. I thought it was pretty cool seeing how everything was coming together.

Unfortunately Dad noticed that I was interested in what was happening outside, and that put an IDEA into his head.

Dad said this project was a good opportunity for me to learn from REAL professionals and to pick up skills I could use down the road.

I wasn't really on board with that plan, though.

Most of those builders look like they've got really rough hands from working with all that heavy equipment. But I use all sorts of lotions and creams to make my hands nice and SOFT.

And I'd like to KEEP them that way, because my hands are my best feature.

But that was EXACTLY the wrong thing to tell my dad, because it earned me a one-way ticket outside.

I don't know why Dad sent ME out there and not Rodrick. Manny actually wanted to go WITH me, but Dad told him he was too YOUNG to help. And Manny didn't take it that well.

Dad told me I needed to find the person in charge and see how I could pitch in. So I asked around, and someone introduced me to the FOREMAN, who was in his trailer.

I guess the foreman was too busy to deal with some middle-school kid, so he told me to go and find a guy named Buddy and talk to HIM.

Well, Buddy was pretty easy to find, especially since his name was tattooed on his forehead.

Buddy was working with some guys on the frames for the walls, so I thought I'd start off by telling them who I WAS. But they weren't as impressed as I THOUGHT they should be.

I told these guys I was out there to HELP them. So Buddy told me he had a REALLY important job, which was to hold up a wall they had just framed.

And I DID feel pretty important for a while, at least until I saw that the wall was holding ITSELF up on its own.

Once I understood it was a PRANK, I figured this is just the way builders joke around with one another. So I picked up a hammer and asked Buddy if I could nail some boards together or something.

Buddy told me that would be GREAT, but I was holding a LEFT-handed hammer, and I needed to go and find a RIGHT-handed one.

So I asked around the site, and it took me a long time to realize THAT was a joke, too.

It hit me that since I was the youngest guy out there, the other builders didn't RESPECT me.

I figured they wanted me to QUIT, but I didn't want to give them that SATISFACTION.

I decided I was gonna PROVE myself by working hard, and move up the ranks. And maybe within a week or two I'd have guys like Buddy reporting to ME.

So I went around the construction site finding things I could do to help out. I filled some buckets with water for the builders who were mixing concrete, and I moved a pile of gravel out of the way when a lorry needed to get through.

HONK
HONK

By the time we broke for lunch, I was feeling pretty GOOD about myself. But I didn't want to kick back and relax, because then these guys would think I was LAZY.

So when lunch was delivered, I went around the site handing out everyone's orders. And that made me REALLY popular.

One guy named Luther was in the middle of mixing a batch of concrete, so I had to wait before I could hand him his meatball sub. And to be extra helpful, I unwrapped it for him so he'd be able to have it as soon as he was finished.

But I wasn't being CAREFUL, and the meatballs slid out of the sub and into a bucket of wet concrete.

Luther didn't look like the kind of guy who'd be happy about a meatball sub with no MEATBALLS in it. So I tossed the REST of the sub into the bucket and backed away.

And I'm glad I got out of there when I DID, too. Because when Luther accused Buddy of stealing his meatball sub, things got UGLY.

I snuck back to the house, then locked the door behind me. And, when Dad asked me why I wasn't still out there WORKING, I told him I'd RETIRED.

<u>Sunday</u>

Things were really moving along with the extension until our NEIGHBOURS started complaining.
Mr Larocca had an issue with the NOISE, because he works the night shift at a hospital and needs to sleep during the day.

So Mom's been asking the builders to try and keep it down, but that's not easy to do when you're dealing with HAMMERS.

Our other next-door neighbour, Mrs Tuttle, isn't happy about the extension, EITHER.

Apparently one of the builders rolled a wheelbarrow on to her property and trampled on some of her flowers, and now she wants us to REPLACE them.

And it's not just our NEXT-DOOR neighbours, either. Mrs Rutkowski lives diagonally across the street, and I guess one of her cats got into our yard and stepped on a nail. So she told Dad he had to pay the VET'S bill.

All this complaining is just slowing things down and making the project take LONGER. So the only person who's actually making any PROGRESS around here is MANNY.

He found a toy toolbox in the basement, and he took some scrap wood out of the skip. I'm not exactly sure what he's building in the backyard, but it looks pretty IMPRESSIVE.

The skip is definitely the best thing about this project. Whenever the waste-paper basket in my bedroom gets full, I just empty it into the skip, which is right outside my window.

DUMP

ABC DISPOSAL

What's even better than THAT is how easy it is now when I have to put the trash out on Sunday night. It's my job to put trash stickers on all the bags, then take everything down to the kerb. And that's a giant pain, especially when it RAINS.

RUMBLE RUMBLE

But, with the skip, I don't even have to deal with the STICKERS. I can just chuck the bags straight in.

Tonight I made a pretty stupid mistake, though. I didn't feel like taking each bag out of the trash can, so I tried to empty it into the skip all at once.

Unfortunately I didn't realize how HEAVY the trash can was, and I couldn't get it all the way over the top of the skip. So the whole can tipped backwards, and the trash emptied out of the bags.

So now there was trash EVERYWHERE, and I had to scoop it all back into the bags.

To make matters WORSE, it was a windy night, so the trash was blowing EVERYWHERE. And it wasn't a lot of fun trying to chase all that stuff down in the dark.

I spent an hour picking trash out of Mr Larocca's bushes. But I should've remembered that he works the night shift and leaves at that time.

<u>Monday</u>

I got to bed super late yesterday, because I had to try and convince Mr Larocca that I wasn't toilet-papering his bushes.

I REALLY wish I had got a good night's sleep, though, because we had a big test at school this morning, and I don't think I did my best.

This was one of those tests the whole SCHOOL has to take. The teachers have been trying to get us ready for WEEKS, because apparently the results really MATTER.

I guess our school did really badly on this test LAST year, and if that happens AGAIN there are gonna be budget cuts. And that means some teachers could lose their JOBS.

On top of that, they might have to cut some subjects, like Art and Music. I wish KIDS had a say in what to cut, because if I was the one making the calls Phys Ed would've been on the chopping block a long TIME ago.

The teachers have been really stressed out about this test, and the last few weeks haven't been a lot of FUN.

All this pressure has been getting us KIDS stressed out, too, so last week the school brought a Stress Puppy into the library to help everyone relax. But kids got too grabby with the puppy, and then the PUPPY got all stressed out.

The puppy started running round in circles and peeing all over the place. So the school took it away and replaced it with a Stress Lizard, and nobody wanted to TOUCH that thing.

Speaking of stress, I really wasn't looking forward to going home this afternoon, because I knew they were gonna cut a hole in the wall to connect it to the extension.

I was worried they might accidentally have to cut through the PLUMBING, and I didn't wanna be around when THAT happened.

Rodrick thought they were gonna use a
WRECKING BALL to smash through the wall,
and his whole plan was to make a music video with
his band when they DID.

So Rodrick and his bandmates were pretty disappointed when they got there and the builders had already opened the wall with a power saw.

I didn't see any sign of the Grout, so THAT was a relief. But what the builders found inside the walls was just as BAD.

The wood underneath the cladding was ROTTEN, because of a leak caused by the clogged gutters. And apparently there was toxic mould in the walls, so we've been living with THAT all this time, too.

Plus, there were rodents' nests in the walls, which means we've been sharing our house with a colony of MICE.

It really creeps me out to think there's this whole WORLD living inside our walls without us even knowing. And that's why I've decided when I build my first house it's gonna be 100% GLASS.

<u>Friday</u>
Ever since they opened up that wall, we've been finding mouse droppings on our kitchen counters. So that means the mice are living out in the OPEN now.

Mom says we can't leave any food lying around, because then the mice will get up on the surfaces where we EAT. So we've been trying to keep everything really CLEAN, and I've been putting our snacks in places where the mice can't get them.

Dad's been looking up ways to get rid of mice that won't HURT them. But Rodrick has his OWN ideas for what to do. He wants to buy a SNAKE and let nature take its course.

When Mom asked Rodrick what we'd do once the snake had eaten the MICE, he said we'd buy a MONGOOSE to catch the snake. So remind me not to visit RODRICK'S house when I'm older.

The mice aren't our ONLY problem, though. We've got WASPS in the house now, too. Mom found one crawling on the mantel above the fireplace last night, and there was another one flying around the kitchen this morning during BREAKFAST.

BZZZZZ

We can't figure out how they're getting INSIDE,
because we've been keeping the windows shut and
we don't open the front door unless we HAVE to.

Mom thinks they might be coming in from
underneath the tarp that's covering the side of
the house, so she sent Dad out there tonight to
make sure there aren't any gaps where they're
getting through.

But Dad wasn't happy about it, because there was
a THUNDERSTORM.

I would've HELPED him, but I was afraid of being struck by LIGHTNING. At school, Albert Sandy told us about this kid who got hit by lightning while he was out in a canoe, and now he's SUPERCHARGED with electricity.

Well, everyone at my lunch table thought that sounded pretty COOL, but I know that, if it happened to ME, everyone would just use me as a charging station.

Rodrick had a theory about how the wasps were getting in, but it sounded kind of CRAZY.

He explained there are lots of different TYPES of wasp, like paper wasps and mud wasps. He said we've probably got SEWER wasps, and they're getting in through the TOILETS.

Well, I've never heard of a sewer wasp before, but I'm not taking any CHANCES.

Right now we've got a rodent problem and an insect problem, and I'm not sure which is WORSE. I don't know why our house can't be infested with something CUTE instead. Because if we were overrun by KOALAS I really wouldn't have a problem with it.

Saturday

Last week the builders had to disconnect our air conditioner so they could bring in a bigger unit. So for now we're all sleeping in the basement, because that's the only place in the house where it's COOL.

I can see why Rodrick likes it down there, ESPECIALLY in the summer. I don't love being underground, though, which is making me rethink the whole plan for my dream house.

Dad said, when he was growing up, some people built BUNKERS where they could go if there was a war or something.

Well, living in a tiny underground space with my whole family sounds like a TERRIBLE idea. First of all, the snacks would be gone by the second day. And if we only had one toilet down there, we'd have MAJOR problems.

I guess we'd have a periscope so we'd know when the coast was clear on the surface. But if the periscope got BLOCKED we might never know it was OK to go back UP.

Dad said some people still build bunkers so they can stay safe if there's a natural disaster, like a TORNADO or something. Well, this morning I thought we were experiencing an EARTHQUAKE, and the LAST place I wanted to be was underground.

But the reason the ground was shaking was because the builders were outside JACKHAMMERING.

RATATATAT

They were breaking up our OLD driveway so they could pour a NEW one, and I was pretty sure the neighbours weren't gonna be happy about all the NOISE. Especially Mr Larocca, who had just got home from his shift at the hospital.

RATAT ATATAT

But I was EXCITED about the new driveway.
Our old one was in really bad shape, so you
couldn't really USE it for anything. And maybe
that's what's been holding me back from becoming
a professional athlete all this time.

When they hauled the rubble away and the lorry
came to pour the fresh concrete, I started to
get NERVOUS.

A lot of the kids in my neighbourhood are
JERKS, and if they see wet concrete they'll
write stupid stuff in it.

On top of that, Mrs Rutkowski's CATS have been in our yard a lot lately hunting for MICE, and I didn't want a bunch of paw prints in the freshly poured concrete.

So, after the builders finished, I patrolled the perimeter to make sure everyone stayed OFF.

PAT
PAT

I was watching the STREET, but it turns out I should've been watching the GARAGE.

I heard the door open, and Rodrick started reversing his VAN out. I tried to STOP him, but he was playing his music too loud to hear.

I couldn't BELIEVE no one in the house had told him about the driveway. But it turns out they had a really good excuse, because they were dealing with a more SERIOUS problem.

SMOKE was pouring out of the windows on the ground floor, and I heard SIRENS in the distance.

Mom came running out of the front door, and
Dad was right behind her.

Ten seconds later a FIRE ENGINE pulled up at
the kerb, and a couple of firefighters got out.

REEEEEEEEEEEEEEEE

They ran across the lawn and on to the front path, which the builders had just finished pouring.

That's when everyone realized that MANNY was still inside. But thankfully he'd already had PRACTICE for this sort of thing.

The GOOD news is, there wasn't actually a FIRE, there was just a lot of SMOKE. But the bad news is, it was MY fault.

Last week, when we were putting our food in places where the mice couldn't get at it, I hid some snacks in the OVEN.

So, when Mom preheated the oven to put in a batch of bacon this morning, a plastic bag MELTED. It's kind of UNFORTUNATE, because that was a waste of some perfectly good crisps.

And this was definitely one of those times when I could've used that escape hatch at the back of my closet.

CAN I CRASH AT YOUR PLACE FOR A WHILE?

Wednesday

Believe it or not, Mom and Dad have already moved past the whole crisp-packet incident. And that's good news for ME.

But the REASON they've forgotten about it is the BAD news.

A few days ago, the building inspector came out to check the framework of the extension.

And, when he DID, he found out the whole structure was too close to Mrs Tuttle's property line by about three FEET.

I guess the construction company messed up when they created the plans for the extension, but the council didn't catch the mistake when they issued the building permit. So now there was just a bunch of finger-pointing, and no one would take any responsibility.

The building inspector told us the only thing we could really do NOW was to get our next-door neighbour to sign something that says we had permission to build the structure close to her property line. But that wasn't gonna be EASY.

The other day, when the concrete guys came back to patch up the driveway and front path, they set up their cement mixer on our lawn. But I guess they forgot we were on a HILL, because the mixer tipped over and poured fresh concrete right into Mrs Tuttle's GARDEN.

So, when Mom and Dad asked for Mrs Tuttle's permission to keep our extension where it WAS, she wasn't looking to do them any favours.

Mrs Tuttle wouldn't BUDGE, and the council told
Mom and Dad the whole structure was gonna have
to come DOWN. And that's exactly what happened
this afternoon.

So now EVERYONE'S unhappy, except for
MANNY. He finished work on HIS place
TODAY, and he had a housewarming party to
celebrate.

JUNE

Thursday

Mom's been in a real funk ever since the extension was torn down.

I figured we'd just start over and build it the RIGHT way this time. But Mom said we'd burned through most of Aunt Reba's inheritance during construction, and we were gonna need to spend the REST patching up the side of the house.

So Mom was ALREADY in a bad mood when my test results came in the post, and they didn't cheer her up any.

It wasn't only MY results that were bad, though. The whole CLASS did poorly, and I can tell you the reason WHY.

During the middle of the test, some kid let the Stress Lizard out of its tank, and it's really hard to CONCENTRATE when there's a REPTILE on the loose.

So I guess this means the school is gonna lose its funding, and Mom's not HAPPY about it.

In fact, she's so upset she's saying we should MOVE so we can live in a better school district.

But nobody ELSE is crazy about moving to another town. Dad grew up here, and he says he doesn't see any REASON to move.

And RODRICK doesn't wanna leave, either. He says his band is FAMOUS in our town, and he doesn't wanna start over somewhere else. But I don't know how famous you can really BE if your last concert was at a bowling alley.

Rodrick says he's NEVER moving, and, even if the REST of us moved out, he'd just keep living in the basement.

And, to be honest with you, I don't think Rodrick would even NOTICE if a new family moved in.

I don't think MANNY'S going anywhere, either. He just put in a sprinkler system, and his yard is really coming on nicely.

Truthfully, I didn't know how I felt about moving. I guess I'm OK with where we live now, but maybe it wouldn't be such a bad idea to start fresh somewhere ELSE.

The great thing about moving is that when you go to a new place you can decide who you wanna BE.

Maybe I could come up with a new LOOK, and people would think I was a "bad boy".

I could even become a whole new PERSON, and tell everyone I'm a professional snowboarder or something.

WHAT'RE YOU DOING THIS WEEKEND?

SHREDDIN' THE GNAR WITH STEEZ, GAPERS!

But maybe I could take it even further than THAT. I could pretend I'm from another COUNTRY where they don't speak English.

And then my teachers would be impressed when I picked up some new phrases.

It's actually kind of FUN imagining a whole new life for myself in a different place.

Back in elementary school, we used to play this game called M.A.S.H., which stands for Mansion, Apartment, Shack, House. I'd write down all the possibilities for my future, and then roll a dice over and over and strike things out until I only had one item left in each category.

I actually found some of my old M.A.S.H. sheets from the fifth grade in my closet a few weeks back.

M.A.S.H.

Home	Location
~~Mansion~~	~~Mountain~~
(Apartment)	(Desert)
~~Shack~~	~~Jungle~~
~~House~~	~~Iceberg~~

Job	Salary
~~Doctor~~	~~$1,000,000~~
(Zookeeper)	~~$100,000~~
~~Plumber~~	($1,000)
~~Magician~~	~~$0~~

Wife	# Kids
~~Holly~~	~~0~~
~~Becky~~	(1)
(Erin)	~~4~~
~~None~~	~~20~~

Whenever I played, I always hoped I'd get a perfect result. But even if I got a good choice in most categories there would always be that one item that ruined EVERYTHING.

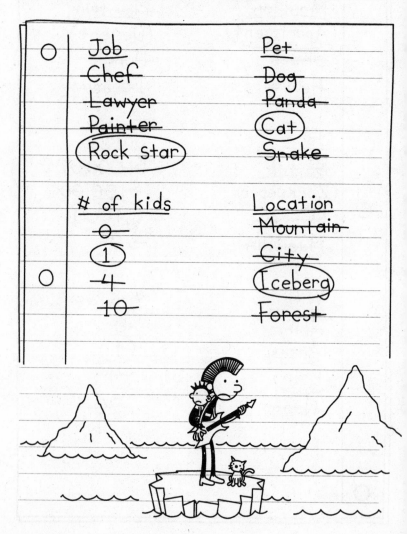

O

Job	Pet
~~Chef~~	~~Dog~~
~~Lawyer~~	~~Panda~~
~~Painter~~	(Cat)
(Rock Star)	~~Snake~~

# of kids	Location
~~0~~	~~Mountain~~
(1)	~~City~~
~~4~~	(Iceberg)
~~10~~	~~Forest~~

O

One of the reasons I liked playing M.A.S.H. so much was because it was a good chance to hang out with the girls at recess. And the girl I liked MOST back then was Becky Anton.

So sometimes I'd cheat a little when I was filling out my M.A.S.H. categories to guarantee I got a good result.

These days, Becky hardly knows who I AM, even though we're lab partners in Biology. I keep thinking I should bring up the fact that we're supposed to get MARRIED one day, but the timing never seems right.

That's ANOTHER good reason to move. I could SERIOUSLY improve my DATING situation. Because if there's one thing girls love, it's the NEW guy.

Kelson Garrity was the new guy at the beginning of this school year. And when he showed up, the girls went CRAZY for him.

Well, it took a few weeks before everyone realized that Kelson was kind of WEIRD, and now the girls won't go NEAR him. But he had a good run for a while there.

So there are probably a LOT of good reasons to move. In fact, the only DOWNSIDE is that I'd need to find a new BEST FRIEND.

And I don't know if that would be WORTH it. I've invested a lot of time and energy into Rowley, and I can't really see myself starting over with someone NEW.

DID YOU KNOW IF YOUR HAND IS BIGGER THAN YOUR FACE IT'S A SIGN OF "LOW INTELLIGENCE"?

REALLLY?

But, if we DO end up moving, I've got a whole list of REQUIREMENTS for a future best friend.

Number ONE, they've got to like WATCHING somebody playing video games more than they like playing games themselves.

Number TWO, it would be nice if they could actually DRAW. Because I'm really into creating comics and stuff.

And, number THREE, they've gotta have junk cereal in their house. I really don't know if I can be friends with another kid whose parents are health nuts.

But, most important, they've gotta have a good sense of HUMOUR. Because, if there's one thing you should know about me, it's that I'm kind of a practical joker.

<u>Saturday</u>

So it turns out Mom is actually SERIOUS about this moving thing. She's been spending time each night looking at different houses online, and I'VE kind of got into it, TOO.

Every place we've looked at so far has some kind of ISSUE, though. There was one house with a big backyard, but it was right near a sewage treatment plant. And there was another one that was brand new, but the house only had one bathroom. Me and Mom were ready to give up looking, but then we found a place that looked PERFECT.

Your Dream Home

3,000 square foot home in desirable neighbourhood. 4 bed, 2.5 bath colonial. Updates include gleaming hardwood floors and modern light fixtures.

The house is just a few years old, and it looks like it's in a nice neighbourhood. But what got MOM most excited was the big KITCHEN.

Mom looked up the local school, and the test scores were pretty good. Then she called the estate agent to find out when we could go and SEE the place.

The estate agent said there was an open house this weekend, and we should drop by if we could. So this morning Mom told everyone to get in the car to check the place out.

Nobody else was HAPPY about that, because, like I said before, the rest of my family doesn't want to MOVE.

But, when we pulled into the neighbourhood, everyone started to change their tune.

The estate agent let our family in and showed us around the house, which was WAY nicer than ours. And the kitchen was even bigger than it looked in the PICTURES.

But what really got my attention was the
SWIMMING POOL in the backyard.

Rodrick and Manny must've spotted it before I
did, because both of them were already out there
by the time I got down the back stairs.

We've been trying to get Mom and Dad to put a pool in our backyard FOREVER. They always tell us that the hot tub is just as GOOD as a pool, but, believe me, it's not the same.

And this was an IN-GROUND pool. We actually had an above-ground pool when I was younger, but it didn't even last a WEEK.

BLOOSH

The estate agent showed us a few more features of the house, but she didn't NEED to because we were already SOLD.

On our way home, everyone was SUPER excited. Rodrick said that he's gonna use the pool to do summer CONCERTS, and it'll be a totally crazy scene every Friday night.

I decided that I'm gonna CHARGE people to come and use our pool, but that I'll make exceptions for CERTAIN people.

But Manny was the most excited of ALL. He's got big plans for the pool, too, and all I can say is, it's gonna take a lot of chocolate PUDDING.

<u>Monday</u>

We had another family meeting last night, and this was a BIG one. Everyone's on board with moving to the new house, so that's great.

Mom told us not to TELL anyone yet, because we still have to sell OUR house so we can afford to buy the NEW one. It was a little hard for me to keep that information to MYSELF, though, and I figured there wouldn't be any harm in telling just ONE person.

But maybe I should've told someone besides ROWLEY, because he didn't take the news too well.

I guess I could've eased Rowley into it instead of hitting him with the information all at once.

I tried to make him feel better by saying we'd stay FRIENDS and that he could come and use my pool on days when it wasn't too CROWDED. But that didn't seem to cheer him up at ALL.

Hopefully Rowley will come round, though, because I'm not sure I can deal with this kind of drama every day.

After dinner tonight, Mom asked her friend who's an estate agent to come over and help us sell OUR house. So we went from room to room, and Mrs Laghari told us what we were gonna have to CHANGE before we could put it on the market.

She said we were gonna need to replace our carpets, give everything a fresh coat of paint and put new tiles in the kitchen and bathrooms. And that was just for STARTERS.

Mrs Laghari said that we'd have to take down our family photos, because buyers like to imagine THEMSELVES living in the house. Well, that was fine with ME, because there are SOME pictures that should've come down a long TIME ago.

Then Mrs Laghari told us that when we have an open house we should lock the basement door so no one sees what's down there.

The last thing Mrs Laghari told us is that most of our furniture was "outdated" and we should probably just cover it up with sheets for the open house. I think that hurt Mom's feelings, and she said people would LOVE her taste in furniture.

But Mrs Laghari said that if we didn't do all the things she recommended she'd have a hard time selling our house. So Mom said in THAT case we'd sell the house OURSELVES, and she showed Mrs Laghari to the door.

I guess this means Mom and Mrs Laghari aren't FRIENDS any more. But that's OK, because we're moving soon ANYWAY.

Sunday
Mom wants to prove our house is great the way it IS, so we're trying to sell it without making any big changes. The open house was this afternoon, but we spent the whole WEEK getting ready for it.

It was MY job to write the description to post online. And I got a little creative to try and make it stand out.

> ## Four-bedroom house with three bathrooms in nice neighbourhood. Home of former bank robber. Possible gold/rare coins buried under floorboards.

We took photos of every room and posted those, too. The house was a MESS when we took the pictures, though, so we had to move some stuff around to make it LOOK clean.

FLASH

The open house started at noon, and we really had to scramble to get everything nice and neat. We did the best we could and got out of there just before people started to arrive.

But it was kind of hard sitting there doing NOTHING while total STRANGERS went into our house.

Mom said none of the people at our open house actually knew we were the OWNERS, so WE could pretend to be checking the place out, TOO. And that way we could listen in on what everyone was saying.

Well, I thought that sounded kind of FUN, so I went inside with Mom. But everyone ELSE in the family thought it was a dumb idea and stayed back in the car.

It turns out the spying idea was a MISTAKE, though. Most of the people didn't have anything NICE to say about our house, and it was kind of tough hearing all the criticism.

But I think Mom was taking it a little harder than I was. Because, whenever someone had something NEGATIVE to say, she'd speak up.

Mom got so upset that she went back out to the CAR. But I stayed in the HOUSE, because I wasn't comfortable with all these random strangers poking around our things.

But not everyone was exploring the house. There were a bunch of men in the family room watching a football game, and, from the look of things, they had helped themselves to our SNACKS.

These guys were letting their kids run wild in our house while they sat back and watched TV. So they were basically using the open house for free BABYSITTING.

Since these dads weren't watching their KIDS, it was up to ME to make sure they didn't BREAK anything.

But I couldn't be everywhere at ONCE, and I was upstairs chasing kids out of our bathroom when there was a loud noise DOWNSTAIRS.

CRASH

It sounded like a kid had tipped over the FRIDGE or something, so I ran down to make sure nobody was HURT. But it wasn't a KID who'd made the noise, it was one of the DADS.

One of the guys had gone into the laundry room looking for more SNACKS, but that's where we were keeping all the stuff we couldn't hide anywhere ELSE.

I guess the noise freaked out the other dads, because they scooped up their kids and left in a HURRY.

So that was the end of the open house, and we didn't get a SINGLE offer.

At dinner tonight, everyone was kind of bummed out. But, while we were doing the dishes, there was a knock on the front door.

It was a couple from out of town. They said they hadn't been able to make it to the open house in time. So Mom invited them in to show them around. They seemed pretty IMPRESSED, and the lady said EXACTLY what Mom wanted to hear.

And, believe it or not, they made an offer right on the spot.

<u>Saturday</u>

I knew I was gonna have to tell Rowley we were selling our house, but I didn't want a repeat of what happened the LAST time we talked about it.

I came up with an idea for how to handle it THIS time around. There's a Preston Platypus book on this EXACT subject, and I figured it was the PERFECT way to get Rowley used to the idea of me moving. So I took the book with me to his house this afternoon.

It felt a little AWKWARD reading a story to Rowley. But I think he's USED to having books read to him, so he made himself comfortable.

I don't really think the message of the book was getting THROUGH to Rowley, though. And the story kind of made me MAD, anyway. It was about how Preston Platypus has a best friend named Pelican Pete, and they do EVERYTHING together.

But then one day Pelican Pete says he's MOVING, and Preston Platypus is sad. And I was FINE with the story up to that point.

Then Preston's mom tells him he'll make NEW friends after Pete moves, and everything will work out for the best. Sure enough, by the end of the book, that's EXACTLY what happens.

And so Preston and his NEW pals had fun all summer long.

THE END

So basically Preston Platypus forgets about Pelican Pete, and all their years of friendship don't mean a THING. And we never find out what happens to Pelican Pete or if he's happy in HIS new neighbourhood.

I thought about writing an angry letter to whoever WROTE this garbage. But of course Rowley LIKED the story, and he wanted me to read him ANOTHER one.

I decided to just stop dancing around the issue and tell Rowley what was REALLY going on. And the second I did I REGRETTED it.

I told Rowley to try not to get too worked up because it wasn't a done deal yet. But nothing I said made any difference.

I had to tell Rowley that if he was gonna be so DRAMATIC I was going HOME.

So then Rowley promised he'd keep himself together, and he DID, but just BARELY.

Maybe it was a mistake telling Rowley about ANY of this. I probably should've sent him a postcard AFTER I moved, because that would've been a lot easier on BOTH of us.

Wednesday
The owners of the house with the pool accepted our offer, so I guess this is really HAPPENING.

The people who are buying OUR place had a home survey done over the weekend, and they found a few things we're gonna have to fix before they'll buy the house. The most SERIOUS issue was a problem with the ceiling underneath Mom and Dad's shower.

Apparently that clogged drain was a bigger problem than we THOUGHT. The floorboards under the bathroom tiles were totally rotten, so now we're gonna have to REPLACE them.

We're lucky nothing TERRIBLE ever happened. Because I can think of things even worse than the GROUT.

The other thing the buyers want us to do is get rid of the HOT TUB, because they have young kids and they're worried about SAFETY. And I'm 100% with them on THAT one.

Now I know for SURE that we're moving, I have a TOTALLY different attitude to school. Since it's almost summer, I asked Mom if I could SKIP classes for the rest of the year.

But she said if I don't go to school they could throw her and Dad in JAIL. I thought about whether or not that would be WORTH it, but I decided I could just suck it up for a little while longer.

I realized that next year I won't be going to school with these kids, and that's what gave me the courage to finally tell Becky Anton that I LIKED her. So during Biology I told Becky I'd had a crush on her ever since fifth grade.

But Becky went straight to the TEACHER, and five minutes later I had a new lab partner. And I'm seriously thinking about the JAIL option again, because I don't know if I can last the rest of the school year dealing with Kelson Garrity.

That's not even my WORST problem, though.
Ever since I told Rowley that we're officially
MOVING, he's been a total MESS. Even
though he keeps promising he's not gonna go all
BLUBBERY on me, the smallest thing can set
him off.

And, even when he IS keeping it together,
he still says these little things that make me
feel GUILTY about moving.

On the way home from school today, we had to walk on the grass because they'd just repaved the pavement. But that gave Rowley an IDEA. He said we should write our NAMES in the cement with a stick and put "BEST FRIENDS" underneath.

It made me a little uncomfortable writing in something so PERMANENT, though, especially since I didn't know what the friend situation would be in my new neighbourhood. I didn't wanna mention that to Rowley, though, because I knew it would set him off again.

So I wrote some extra stuff with the stick to give me a little wiggle room, just in case.

Greg & Rowley
BEST
FRIENDS*

* currently

Saturday

School ended a week ago and, while everyone ELSE is already enjoying their summer holiday, we've been PACKING.

TOSS

Mom created a binder and a schedule for everyone in the family, and we're all responsible for boxing up our own stuff. It's gonna be TIGHT, but we should be done by the time the moving lorries show up next weekend.

The person who's taking the LONGEST is DAD. He wants to make sure none of his Civil War figurines break, so he's using a whole roll of bubble wrap for each ONE.

Mom's been hoping our neighbours would throw us a going-away party, but, with all the construction over the past month, we're not that POPULAR around here. So Mom decided we'd just throw a party for OURSELVES.

The party was TONIGHT. We'd sent out invitations to just about everyone on our street, and we set everything up in our yard.

Rodrick was excited, because Mom and Dad were letting his band play, and they were even PAYING him. We were still busy setting up when the first guests started to arrive.

I wasn't sure if I should even INVITE Rowley to the party, because I was afraid he might have another breakdown. But I was actually really happy to see him.

His parents seemed happy, TOO, and I almost got the feeling they were GLAD I was moving.

Rowley said he had a GIFT for me, which was a giant collage with a bunch of pictures of us over the years. And, I'm not gonna lie, it got me a little choked up.

I was kind of RELIEVED that's all Rowley's gift was. Because the way he's been acting lately, I wouldn't be surprised if he gave me one of his FINGERS or something.

Rowley said I could hang the collage in my NEW bedroom to remind me of all the fun stuff we did together. And I don't know if there was a lot of pollen in the air tonight or WHAT, but right then I think I got something in my eye.

Things were getting a little too touchy-feely for me, though, so I was glad when more people started to arrive at the party.

It picked up really FAST from there. Rodrick's band started playing out on the back deck, and the music attracted some teenagers who were at a high-school graduation party a few doors down. Then it seemed like everyone on our street was at our party all at ONCE, and it got CRAZY.

Our party was pretty WILD, but it was
NOTHING compared to MANNY'S. And his
party was still going strong when I turned in for
the night.

Sunday
I have to admit, last night was a lot of FUN.
But I'm kind of SAD, because just when things
are getting GOOD around here we're LEAVING.

I was the first one in the house awake today,
and when I looked out of the window, I knew we
were in for a long day of clean-up.

I wished we still had that SKIP, because that would've made things a whole lot EASIER.

While I was looking over the front lawn, two big moving lorries pulled up at the kerb. I was kind of CONFUSED, because our move was still a week away.

A few guys got out of the lorries, and one of them came to our front door. So I went out to MEET him.

The man told me his team was ready to start
putting our stuff into the lorries, and they needed
to come into the house. By now, Mom had come
downstairs and was at the front door.

She told the guy that he was a week EARLY,
and that the move wasn't until NEXT Sunday.
But he pulled out a contract that showed
TODAY'S date as the moving day, and it had
Mom's SIGNATURE at the bottom.

Mom told the guy she'd made a MISTAKE, and
that we weren't READY to move yet. He told
her the deposit was "non-refundable" and that if
we didn't move TODAY we'd lose the money we'd
already paid.

Now Mom was in a PANIC. She woke everyone up and told us to get PACKING. The movers said we had a two-hour window to get everything on to the lorries, so we really had to HUSTLE.

Up to this point we'd been really careful packing so nothing got DAMAGED. But now there was no TIME for that.

The movers REALLY didn't care if our stuff got broken. And that's why it was probably a bad idea to let them pack up our DISHES.

Mom asked the movers to just focus on the FURNITURE instead, and they went down to the basement to start there.

Then someone rang the doorbell. It was the guy we'd hired to take the HOT TUB away, and his crane was parked in our front yard.

With everything ELSE going on in the house, this was pretty terrible TIMING.

The crane operator explained that he couldn't get his vehicle into our backyard without running over our neighbour's flower garden, so his plan was to lift the hot tub OVER the house.

That sounded a little crazy to ME, but I figured this guy probably knew what he was doing.

I showed the guy where the hot tub was, and he put some straps around it. Then he attached the straps to a giant HOOK and lifted the hot tub off the deck.

But when he tried to reverse his vehicle, he COULDN'T, because the movers had piled up a bunch of FURNITURE in our yard. So now the hot tub was dangling above our ROOF.

As if the whole situation wasn't stressful enough
ALREADY, all of a sudden ROWLEY showed up
in my front yard.

But I didn't have TIME to deal with Rowley, because now I had a NEW problem.

That guy from Whirley Street had pulled up in front of our house, and he was taking the FURNITURE that the movers had left by the kerb. And that's when I remembered it was SUNDAY, which is the day we leave our TRASH out.

I tried to wave the guy off to make him go away. But the crane operator thought I was giving him a signal that it was OK to reverse his vehicle, which is what he DID.

And that was the end of our living-room COUCH.

The CRANE stopped, but the hot tub DIDN'T.
It started swinging in crazy circles above the
house, and then it slammed into our CHIMNEY.

The bricks slid off the roof and just missed my
PARENTS, who had come outside to see what all
the COMMOTION was.

After that, I thought it was OVER, because I
couldn't imagine anything ELSE happening. But
something DID.

Some wasps had built a nest in our CHIMNEY,
which explains how they'd been getting into the
house all this time. And now they were LOOSE,
looking for REVENGE.

We all ran for cover inside the house, but the crane
operator wasn't quick enough to get away.

The wasps flew into the cabin of his vehicle, which made him kick the lever that released the HOT TUB, which fell through the ROOF.

And at that point, to tell the truth, I was kind of RELIEVED. Because now I knew for SURE that things really couldn't get any WORSE.

Thursday

There was one bright spot from what happened over the weekend, and it's that Rodrick made it through the experience ALIVE.

The hot tub landed smack in the middle of his BEDROOM, so we thought he'd got CRUSHED. But, when the movers had hauled Rodrick's bed out of the basement, they loaded it on to one of the lorries and took him WITH it.

Everything else is BAD news. The people who were supposed to buy OUR house pulled out, and that meant we couldn't afford the NEW one. So I guess that means we're STUCK here for a while.

To be honest with you, I'm not totally sure I was ready to move, anyway. Looking for a new best friend would've been a huge hassle, and, besides, there's so much more I need to TEACH Rowley before I go.

There's probably a LESSON I could learn from this whole experience, like "be happy with what you've got" or "there's no place like home" or that sort of thing. But that's the kind of corny stuff they put in books for little kids.

So here's the lesson I'M taking away from all this: don't be late for an old lady's funeral. Because, believe me, she'll make you PAY.

ACKNOWLEDGEMENTS

Thanks to my wife, Julie, for your love and support, especially during my deadlines. Thanks to my family for cheering me on all these years.

Thanks to Charlie Kochman for caring about every period, comma, and semicolon in these books. Thanks to everyone at Abrams, including Michael Jacobs, Andrew Smith, Hallie Patterson, Melanie Chang, Kim Lauber, Mary O'Mara, Alison Gervais, and Elisa Gonzalez. Thanks also to Susan Van Metre and Steve Roman.

Thanks to my awesome, friendly Wimpy Kid team: Shaelyn Germain, Anna Cesary, and Vanessa Jedrej. Thanks to Deb Sundin, Kym Havens, and the incredible staff at An Unlikely Story.

Special thanks to Chad W. Beckerman for your outstanding design skills and for your friendship over these many years. Thanks to Liz Fithian for all the great memories on our travels.

Thanks to Rich Carr and Andrea Lucey for your outstanding support. Thanks to Paul Sennott for all your help. Thanks to Sylvie Rabineau and Keith Fleer for everything you do for me.

As always, thanks to Jess Brallier for your continued support.

ABOUT THE AUTHOR

Jeff Kinney is a #1 *New York Times* bestselling author and a six-time Nickelodeon Kids' Choice Award winner for Favourite Book. Jeff has been named one of *Time* magazine's 100 Most Influential People in the World. He is also the creator of Poptropica, which was named one of *Time*'s 50 Best Websites. He spent his childhood in the Washington, D.C., area and moved to New England in 1995. Jeff lives with his wife and two sons in Massachusetts, where they own a bookstore, An Unlikely Story.

Feeling sneaky?

Check out this EXCLUSIVE EXTRACT from

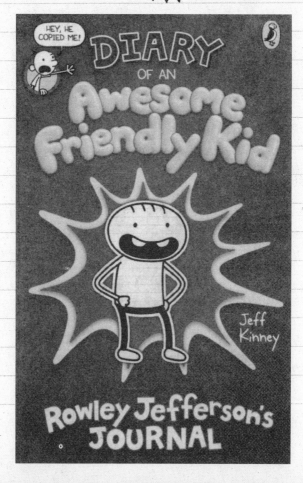

THE TIME ME AND GREG CAME UP
WITH OUR OWN SUPERHERO

Me and Greg were bored one day, and
Mrs Heffley gave us some paper and
markers to draw with.

Then Greg had an AWESOME idea.
He said we should create our own
SUPERHERO.

Greg said the FIRST thing we needed to
do was figure out what kind of POWERS
our superhero should have.

I said maybe he could fly or have super strength but Greg said both those ideas were dumb because they've been done a million times before.

Then I said maybe our superhero could have X-ray vision but Greg said that wasn't a good superpower because once he accidentally saw his grandpa naked and he wishes he HADN'T.

Greg said we needed to do something ORIGINAL so we started coming up with ideas that no one had ever THOUGHT of before. And the ideas we came up with were OK but not great.

The one we liked the best was this guy
called the Chuckster who could throw his
own HEAD like a football.

But Greg said the Chuckster wouldn't
work as an action figure because the head
would be a choking hazard for little kids.

Then we tried to come up with some characters that WOULD be OK if a kid accidentally swallowed them but most of our ideas weren't that good.

Greg said moms are usually the ones who buy their kids toys so we should come up with something THEY'D like. But we weren't happy with that idea either.

Greg said maybe the reason we weren't coming up with anything good was that we weren't a very good TEAM. He said we should each try working on our OWN and see who could come up with a better idea.

We both did our own thing and then we showed each other our work.

Greg's superhero was a guy from space who had a different kind of power in each fingertip which was actually a pretty awesome idea.

I told Greg his idea was cool and we should go with THAT.

Then Greg said well what's YOUR idea? But I didn't wanna tell him because I knew he'd laugh. And then he promised he WOULDN'T laugh so I showed him my character.

Greg asked what Amazing Guy's superpower was and I said it was KINDNESS. And that made Greg break his promise about not laughing.

Greg said a superhero should be EDGY and it would be cool if Amazing Guy had knives coming out of his knuckles and wore a black leather jacket and said swears when he fights the bad guys.

But I said I wanted Amazing Guy to be a role model for children, and that made Greg break his promise a second time.

POUND
POUND

Get ready to see the Wimpy world
in a whole new way!

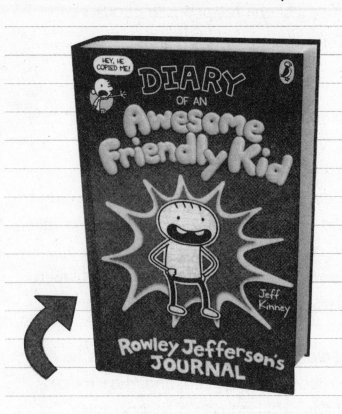

Now it's Rowley's turn to give
HIS side of the story . . .

DIVE INTO
THE DEEP END

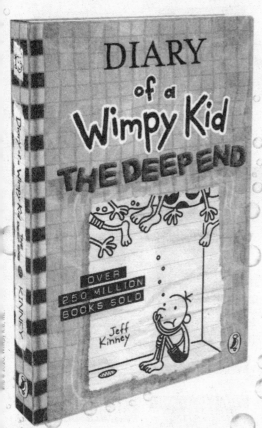

Don't miss the
BRAND-NEW
Diary
of a
Wimpy Kid
BOOK
from
No. 1 international
bestselling author

Jeff Kinney

Have you read them all?

THE ONE WHERE IT ALL BEGINS

THE ONE WITH THE BIG BROTHER

THE ONE WHERE GREG SHAPES UP

THE ONE WITH THE WORST SUMMER EVER

THE ONE WHERE GREG GETS 'THE TALK'

THE ONE WITH THE CRAZY SNOW STORM

THE ONE WITH
THE VALENTINE'S
DANCE

THE ONE WHERE
GREG NEEDS
A NEW FRIEND

THE ONE WITH THE
FAMILY ROAD TRIP

THE ONE WITH THE
SCARY SCHOOL TRIP

THE ONE WHERE
GREG AND ROWLEY
MAKE A
HORROR FILM

THE ONE WITH
THE HOLIDAY
DISASTER

THE ONE WITH
THE WINTER
BATTLE

THE ONE WITH THE
HEFFLEYS' HOME
DISASTER

THE ONE THAT
ROWLEY WROTE

Wimpy Kid CLUB

www.wimpykidclub.co.uk

- Watch TONS of cool videos

- Enter AWESOME competitions

- Take the WIMP WARS challenge!

- Read EXTRACTS from the books

- Download must-have FREEBIES!

Sign up for the newsletter
to get ALL the latest
Wimpy Kid gossip FIRST!